"Ready or not, here we come!" Zak's voice echoed.

"Hurry!" said Emmy. "We don't want Zak and Wheezie to f[...]

Emmy led Max into the forest. Instantly they were surrou[...] spooky-looking plants and trees. Emmy felt nervous, even though Quetzal, the dragons' teacher, had told them that the forest was safe.

All around them, flowers glowed. They soon passed the glimmering star tree.
"We're going to get lost," Max said worriedly.
Emmy tried to sound brave. "Just follow me," she said.

Emmy found the perfect hiding place under the star tree. But after a while, Max got tired of hiding.

"The game's over by now," he said. "Let's go back."

Emmy grinned and said, "I bet we won!" Then she stood up and took Max's hand. "C'mon! It's this way."

"Hey, isn't there only one star tree in this forest?" Max asked a few minutes later. Emmy nodded. "Then why are we passing it again?" Max sounded worried.

Emmy realized something was wrong. She stopped and stared at the tree.

"Didn't we come from there?" Emmy said, spinning around.
"Or was it there?" Suddenly nothing felt familiar.
"I think we're lost," Max said.

Emmy knew she had to be brave for Max. "Don't worry—we're in Dragon Land! Nothing bad will happen," she said. "Let's be quiet and think." Max nervously crunched his foofle flower seeds.

"I've got it!" Emmy cried. "We'll leave a trail of foofle flower seeds to keep us from walking in circles."

"Just like Hansel and Gretel," Max said, sounding cheered.

"Max, you can make the trail," Emmy said as they walked along. Suddenly, Emmy heard a strange sound. "What was that?" she whispered. She and Max turned to see some birds gulping down the seeds and tweeting with delight. "They're eating our trail!" Emmy cried.

"Just like in 'Hansel and Gretel,'" Max said glumly.

Emmy tried to remember what her parents had told her to do if she ever got lost. "Don't worry about the trail, Max. We're supposed to stay in one place anyway so it's easier for the others to find us," Emmy said.

"But can we stay next to the star tree?" Max asked. "It's not so dark here."

"I bet the dragons can see this tree when they fly over the forest," Emmy said. "Max! That gives me an idea! Everyone must be looking for us. We could spell a word with glowing star seeds, telling them we're here!"

"Kind of like using a flashlight to signal!" Max said happily. He jumped up and began gathering star seeds. Emmy helped.

"Emmy, can we please write my name?" Max begged. "It's the only word I know how to spell."

"Definitely," she answered.

Max was thrilled. Working together, they spelled out M–A–X in big, glowing letters.

At that very moment, the dragons were flying over the Forest of Darkness, searching for their friends. They had asked Quetzal to help them find Emmy and Max.

"Look!" Zak and Wheezie shouted, spotting the shining seeds.

When the dragons landed beside the star tree, Max and Emmy cheered.

"It's all my fault we got lost," Emmy explained to her friends.

"Well, hiding here was not such a good idea, niña," Quetzal said calmly.

"But staying put and making the glowing message was very smart."

Emmy grinned at her brother. "Max helped," she said.
"Can we get out of here now, pleeeease?" Max pleaded.
And as the children climbed on the backs of their
dragon friends, Max and Emmy sighed in relief.

"Do you still want to play hide-and-seek?" Ord asked.

"Sure, if Max and I can be 'it' together," Emmy replied.

"Why's that, Emmy?" Quetzal asked.

Emmy hugged Max. "We're just like Zak and Wheezie," she said, smiling. "Together, we make a really great team."